So Few of Me

Peter H. Reynolds

WALKER BOOKS

AND SUBSIDIARIES

LONDON • BOSTON • SYDNEY • AUCKLAND

Leo was a busy lad.

However hard he worked,
there was always more to do.

Maybe making a list would help.

Leo's list of things to do
grew longer and longer.

"So few of me and so much to do.
If only there were TWO of me."

Just then, there was a
knock at the door.

Leo opened the door . . .
and blinked and rubbed his eyes —
it was another HIM!

The new Leo snatched
the list and said,
"Two of us will get it done."

The new Leo WAS helpful but he found even MORE jobs to do.
A third Leo joined the other two,
but they still couldn't get everything done.

How about a fourth Leo? Four makes a fantastic team.

But maybe a fifth would be even better.

Five Leos were still not enough.
A sixth came in to help organize them all.
After a long meeting, they decided
they needed a seventh.

With seven Leos, there was
seven times as much work!

Leo himself sighed and said,
"We'll need eight just to catch our breath."

The eight Leos worked furiously.

Would nine Leos get everything done?

No.
Add one more Leo to make ten,
each one busier than the next.

Leo, Leo, Leo, Leo, Leo, Leo, Leo, Leo, Leo,
and Leo stopped to look over their list of things to do.
"Back to work!" shouted nine Leos.

"No time to stop, no time to rest!"
But Leo himself was exhausted.
He slipped away to have a nap.

Leo awoke to nine other Leos staring at him.
"WHAT are you doing?" they demanded.

"I was dreaming," said Leo softly.
"Dreaming was NOT
on the list!" they roared.

Leo smiled, still savouring his dream.
The Leos disappeared one by one.

Leo wondered,
"What if I did less—
but did my BEST?"

"Then <u>one</u> Leo is all that I need.
Just me, just one . . . with time to dream."